Bob
The Bumblebee

Nancy P Best

Written by Nancy Pulling Best
Illustrated by Mathew S. Capron

Bob The Bumblebee

by Nancy Pulling Best
Copyright © 2017

First Paperback Printing, May 2017
Second Paperback Printing, February 2023

Illustrations and Illustration Editing by Mathew S. Capron
Raleigh, North Carolina

Published by
PETRIE PRESS
A Division of Nancy Did It
2985 Powell Road
Blossvale NY 13308
nandidit@twcny.rr.com

Printed in the United States of America
by Versa Press

ISBN 978-0-9711638-7-4

Dedications

This book is dedicated to the kids in my life. My children and grand-children have always been fans of my stories. It was my oldest child who encouraged me to make my "Anna The Spider" poem into a book. She even hooked me up with my illustrator. My youngest grandchildren are the inspiration for this book. They each have an imaginary friend named Bob and they just love the *Transformers* especially Bumblebee. So with a little imagination I present to you "Bob The Bumblebee."

Nancy Pulling Best

Nathan and Matthew Best

To my wonderful daughter who is always busy as a bee. She reminds me to continue to live life to the fullest. Also, my loving wife because she is simply the best.

Mathew S. Capron

Bob was a bumblebee.
He was fluffy and
so fat.

Bob was good looking. He was yellow with some black.

He looked soft and cuddly, but he never got a hug.

Kids were always frightened of this kind of bug.

Bob knew he had a stinger, but he would never sting.

He liked to use his
talent to whistle
and to sing.

The bee had to gather pollen to satisfy the queen.

But when he was finished he'd hide in an evergreen.

The tree offered protection. A place to sing and hide.

Bob knew that he was getting good and he was filled with pride.

One day two boys were taking a walk near Bob's big tree.

They heard some groovy music like an Elvis wannabee.

The boys listened much closer the song was "I'm All Shook Up." They saw the bee dancing and singing about a buttercup.

They had to get
their Grandma to
listen to the song.
They knew she
loved "The King"
and would want
to sing along.

So they ran back to the house and took Grandma by the hand.

And they all danced
and listened to Bob's
new Elvis band.

MEET THE AUTHOR:
Nancy Pulling Best

Born and raised in the Adirondack mountains in upstate New York, Nancy prides herself in being a 4th generation Adirondacker.

"My great grandparents, grandparents, parents, children and 1st grandchild were all from Old Forge, in the Adirondacks," Best said.

After writing for her own personal use, newspapers and magazines, she brings you her third children's book.

She also authored "Anna The Spider," "Pepper The Dragonfly," "Learning To Cook Adirondack" and "Learning To Cook Adirondack Over An Open Fire." They are all available at www.nancydidit.com

MEET THE ILLUSTRATOR:
Mathew S. Capron

Born and raised in the Adirondack mountains in upstate New York, Mat always had a love for art and found a lot of peace in it.

He is the father of a beautiful daughter, who also enjoys being creative.

"I'm happy to have had an opportunity to illustrate this book," Mat said. "I hope you find happiness and peace within."

Mat also illustrated "Anna The Spider" and "Pepper The Dragonfly." More art and illustrations by M@ can be found at... hew-Art.com

Bob went on singing, Whistling
and shaking about. He also
received many Hugs too...

Maprow

Bumblebee Facts

Globally, there are about 250 species of bumblebees. They are found mostly in the temperate zones of North and South America, and Eurasia.

Bumblebees are documented to pollinate many important food crops. They are also more effective than honey bees at pollinating crops grown in greenhouses.

When most insects are inactive due to cold temperatures bumblebees are able to fly by warming their flight muscles by shivering, letting them raise their body temperature so they can fly.

Instead of starting their own colonies, some bumblebees have evolved to take over another species' colony to rear their young. These 'cuckoo' bees then use the workers from the queen-less colony to feed and care for their offspring.

Some bumblebees are known to rob flowers of their nectar. Nectar robbing is when a bee takes nectar from a flower without touching its reproductive parts (i.e. anthers and/or stigma), usually by biting a hole at the base of the flower.

Bumblebees are effective buzz pollinators of several economically important plants like tomato, bell pepper and eggplant. In buzz pollination bees extract pollen from a flower by vibrating against the flower's anthers, making an audible buzzing noise.

Currently, the Common Eastern bumblebee is the only species being commercially raised for pollination services in North America, despite the fact that it is only native to the eastern U.S. and Canada.

What you can do to help protect bumblebees:

- Plant pollen- & nectar-rich plants in your garden

- Provide habitat for bumblebees

- Buy organic & locally produced food

- Join citizen-science efforts to track bumblebees

- Support bumblebee conservation efforts